THE HEN THAT SAVED
THE WORLD

and Other Norwegian Folk Tales

THE HEN THAT SAVED THE WORLD

and Other Norwegian Folk Tales

Retold by
MARGARET SPERRY

Illustrated by Per Beckman

THE JOHN DAY COMPANY
NEW YORK

Preface

From the lips of "old folks," relatives of mine, in Fredrikstad, Norway, I heard for the first time the tales incorporated in this little book. I was only three years old then, but the stories I loved as a child have remained an undying love with me all my years, and now at last I have translated some of them and cast them into my native language so all who read English may see and understand.

At that distant happy time, fact and fable mingled marvelously: our house was set on the crest of a hill overlooking the sea and meadows where old battles had been waged in a dim and glorious time.

The master of that domain of children, land, and boats was my uncle, a sea captain who related great roaring tales of sea and wreck. He was victim, himself, to both. An end was made of him by heavy storm but his tales go on forever. I have never forgotten them.

Our sojourn in the Norwegian city at an end, my mother took me to live on a farm known as "The Place on the Nose." There I experienced my first unforgettable Christmas. The farmer went on skis into a snowstorm to fetch our tree, and so tall was it, it reached to the very roof. The farmer's wife and my mother made each tree ornament by hand. Decked in its holy day glory, on Christmas Eve, peasants danced round it to sound of harmonica and fiddle! There it was we were made a gift for the Christmas roast of the heart of a real elk shot in the forest.

And there it was my blond beautiful Scandinavian mother

put into my hands my very first book! It was a modest little volume done in shiny marbled paper, and its leaves smelled of needles of the pine. And its contents? A small collection of these very same folk tales in Norwegian!

For years thereafter, through my mother's frequent reading, I seemed to live with the characters described in these old tales: the enchanted cat, the pig of pathos, that prince of malice the fox, and the adorable but stupid bear. "Real life" seemed to retreat, whereas fancy gripped and held my mind. I existed in a fairy world where anything might happen and generally did.

In later life after my marriage, I had the happy fortune of returning to Norway. Drawn by love and memory I turned again to those tales of Asbjornsen and Moe who had garnered so richly the lore of Norwegian valleys.

Was it not inevitable that I, saturated as my imagination is with folk tales of my childhood, should translate and retell at least some of them?

Now rereading and enjoying these stories, they still fire my fancy as of old, but I see in them also great depths which belong not only to Norway but to all the world. The truth to be found in a folk tale proves once again that the hearts of men and man's dreams are the same in all places and time.

MARGARET SPERRY

6

Contents

The Bewitched Cat

NCE upon a time a very poor man and his wife lived in a lonely hut in the woods. They owned but a kettle, a griddle, a cat, and three sons. What the two eldest boys were called I don't know; but the youngest was named Per.

When their parents died, the three boys were to divide what was left. The eldest son took the kettle, the second son got the griddle. Having no choice, Per was given the cat for his own.

Very soon after, the three sons took their worldly goods and set off to try their luck. The eldest went toward the north, carrying the kettle under one arm. The second son walked toward the east, griddle in knapsack.

Per, the youngest looked at his cat that was white of fur and gentle of manner, and said, "How can I leave you behind in this hut to waste away your life?" Then he led off toward the south and the cat followed him.

When Per had walked for some distance over field and through forest, the cat said, "Sit down on the moss under this pine, and I shall go hunting. Whatever I capture, you must take to the king's farm that lies on the hill yonder."

The cat showed the boy an opening through the trees

from which he could view a slope of purple heather, and above that a high hill on the crest of which was spread a farm with many log buildings of a dark brown color.

"In that farmhouse lives a king," explained the cat. "He is both sad and sour. All day long he sits in one chair and believes only what he sees with his very own eyes."

"Why should I go to visit such a king?" asked the lad.

"To me, he is both near and dear," answered the cat. With this remark, the little creature darted off into the shadows and was lost to sight.

Per did not have to wait long before the cat returned, riding between the horns of a reindeer.

"You, who are so small and weak, how could you capture this large animal?" asked Per.

"The less you ask the more you learn!" was the cat's reply. "Listen with care to all I say: lead this animal to the king's farm and straight into the kitchen. When the king comes to view it, tell him the reindeer is a gift from Sir Per. You must not tell who Sir Per really is, nor where he lives! Keep faith, and all will go well!"

Per promised, then led the reindeer in the direction of the hill. When he came to the main house he walked straight into the kitchen followed by the great animal, and no one stopped him for all were astonished.

At once servants ran to tell their master. "A real live reindeer stands in the middle of your kitchen. The boy with him says the animal is a gift!"

"Stuff and nonsense!" sputtered the king.

All the same he got to his feet and went to look.

When he beheld the animal, he asked Per, "Who is the generous man who sends me so fine a gift?"

"Sir Per and none other!"

"Who is Sir Per?"

"My master and a very good master is he!"

"Where does he live?"

"That I dare not answer."

"Stuff and nonsense!" sputtered the king. "But at least you deserve a meal for your trouble!"

So a supper was brought the boy and when his hunger was sated and his legs rested, he returned to the woods and there under a pine, he found his cat carefully licking her paws.

Per told all that had taken place. At the end, the

little creature remarked, "One gift breaks ice, magic's in thrice!"

Not another word would she say to explain.

On the second day, the cat went hunting again and this time she came riding back on the horns of a hart.

All took place as before, and Per led the animal to the king's farm and straight into the kitchen. When the old man saw this second gift, he was less sour than on the first day. This time he wanted more than ever to know who Sir Per really was and where he lived. The lad kept his promise as before, and told nothing except the name of his master.

When he returned to the woods, he found his cat carefully licking her ears.

Of course Per related everything that had taken place and in the end, the little creature remarked, "Two gifts warm the heart, now a third must take part!"

Not another word would she add.

On the third day when the cat went hunting, she came back riding between the antlers of an enormous elk.

"You, who are so small and weak," cried the lad, "how could you capture this great creature?"

"The more you ask the less you learn!" replied the cat. "Do with this elk as with the reindeer and the hart. Say the same words and keep the same silence!"

Per promised as he had promised on the two previous days, and soon he was making his way to the king's farm.

When the servants saw the huge elk standing in their

kitchen, they rushed to the king and shouted, "A real live elk stands in front of your fire! This, too, is a gift from Sir Per!"

"Stuff and nonsense!" sputtered the king. All the same he got to his legs and ran to look. When his very own eyes beheld the enormous animal standing in his kitchen, he was so amazed and excited, he did not know if he were standing on his right foot or his left.

Again the king asked who Sir Per really was and where he lived. Again the lad kept silent.

Then the king exploded. "Since I can't learn who

your master is, nor where he lives, tell him to come to us! We'll give him a welcome he won't forget!"

Now when Per returned to the woods he found his cat asleep under the pine. He wakened her and related all that had taken place.

The cat asked, "But why do you look so sad?"

"What shall we do about Sir Per's visit to the king?"

"*You* must act the part of Sir Per," answered the cat.

"How can I visit the king in the guise of a lord when I have nothing to wear but the rags on my back?"

"No fear and no tear!" warned the cat. "Wait here for three days while I go to that valley where Glede Castle lies."

With this, she darted off into the forest and was lost to sight.

When, indeed, the cat returned, she came riding in a gilded coach drawn by prancing horses, tawny and white. This coach was laden with clothes for Per and never before had he seen their match; they jingled and dripped with gold and were studded with gems.

"When the king asks whence this raiment comes, reply, 'From Glede Castle, but what I have at home is finer far than this.' "

Well disguised, and adorned like a prince, the lad rode to the king's farm. There he was welcomed by servant and master for all believed him to be Sir Per and none other.

"Whence comes such finery?" asked the old king. "I've not seen the like in my whole life!"

"Well enough for journeys abroad, but what I have at home is finer far than this."

"This home of yours—where is it, and what is its name, Sir Per?"

"The name of my castle is Glede, and it lies in a far-away valley," replied the young lad.

The king looked startled, then said, "That is the very castle I dreamed of when I was young, but when my queen died and my little girl vanished I stopped dreaming. Perhaps, Sir Per, you will take me there?"

"Gladly!" the lad replied, and so it was agreed.

When Per returned to the forest, he found his cat sunning herself on a high branch of the pine. He called to her and she leaped down and sat beside him on the moss while he related all that had taken place.

In the end, she asked, "But why do you look so sad, Per?"

"How shall I take the king to a castle I myself have never seen?"

"Wait and see! Magic's in three!" the cat replied and not another word would she add.

The next day, dressed and disguised as Sir Per, the lad rode to the farm. When he met the king, he cried, "Now let us journey to that faraway valley where Glede Castle lies!"

"What I see I believe, but nothing more!" mumbled the old king and slammed his crown on his head. Off they rode, Per leading the way in his coach. But the cat was nowhere to be seen for she was running far ahead, preparing their way.

When the procession had traveled for some time it passed a flock of sheep whose long wool caressed the hill where they grazed.

Already the cat had said to their shepherd, "When the king asks who owns these sheep, you must say they belong to Sir Per." And the shepherd had agreed.

Now when the old king was riding past, he caught sight of the sheep and cried, "Whose sheep are these?"

"They belong to Sir Per!" the shepherd replied.

When the procession had traveled for a still longer distance they came to a herd of cattle with coats so sleek they shone like silk.

Here again the cat had prepared the way.

When the king came riding by and beheld the fat sleek animals, he cried, "Whose cows are these?"

The cowherd replied as the cat had taught, "They belong to Sir Per, of course!"

When the procession had traveled still farther, they came to a herd of horses, perfect in form, smooth of coat, and matched in color.

The cat, always running ahead, had prepared the way even here, so when the king cried out, "Whose horses are these?" the answer came, "They belong to Sir Per! Indeed, what does not?"

At this the king sputtered, "Does Sir Per own the realm and everything in it?"

But no one bothered to answer. Whereupon the old man fell into a dark silence, and said not a word for the rest of the journey.

At length and at last, the king's procession came to the faraway valley where flowers still bloom when summer has died elsewhere in that northern land. In the midst of the valley rose Glede Castle and its gates were three: brass and silver and gold. The walls shone like crystal, and its turrets were tipped with sun.

An old man with snow-white hair and wearing silver livery opened the gates and welcomed them with many a courtly bow.

Once inside the castle, the old king and Sir Per seemed to glide from room to room. Each was more spacious than the one before. Finally they reached a hall decked for a feast.

Here at last the cat appeared to them. When the old king caught sight of her seated at the head of the table, his eyes grew large with wonder.

But Per said not a word.

The cat bade them be seated and they ranged themselves round the great board aglint with silver and glass, and shining with candles. No sooner had servants carried in rare dishes and spread them before the guests, than a loud thumping sound was heard at the gate. All stopped to listen.

Excusing herself, the cat darted out of the hall. Her velvet feet carried her swiftly to the gate. It opened slowly of itself, and this is what she saw: a troll shaped like a man but twice as tall and three times as broad. His head was as large as a boulder. His eyes were dark holes under the cliff of his brow. His black hair was a tangled stubble. His mouth was a shadowy cave.

The troll kept up a hideous roar: "Who sits in my castle? Who drinks my mead? Who eats my meat?"

"Be silent!" commanded the cat. "Turn round! At your back you will see one far stronger than yourself!"

The troll turned just in time for a strong shaft of sunlight to strike him full in the eyes. As everyone knows, no troll of darkness can live in the sun.

As the beam shone into his eyes, a dreadful change took place: he became even larger than before. Bigger and bigger he grew till his head seemed to fill the sky! Then with a loud explosion his body flew into bits, and within a few moments all that was left of him was a cloud of dust.

"One, two, three! Fate ended thee!" whispered a voice. But it was the voice of the cat no longer. Most curious of all, a change had come over the little creature just as the troll exploded.

Instead of the little animal with white fur and velvety

paws, there appeared now a lovely blond maiden in robe of blue and silver, with a crown of white flowers in her hair, and golden shadows over her blue eyes.

This beautiful young maiden walked slowly back into the castle. When she entered the banquet hall, and the old king beheld her, his mouth fell open, and he sputtered, "She's my very own child! My own long-lost daughter!"

The girl walked swiftly toward him, and put her soft arms round his neck. In a clear sweet voice, she said, "Yes, you are my father! When my mother died, a wicked troll snatched me away. When I refused to marry him he turned me into a white cat and cast me out into the world. But I had the good fortune to find a home with the family of Per. When Per's parents died, and we two went wandering, I knew you and I, Father, would meet once again!"

"So," the king cried, "it was you, Daughter, who sent Per to lift me from sorrow and bring me to this castle?"

"Through Per and none other do we meet again," the princess replied, "and he has captured my heart."

"B-but," stammered Per, "how can I woo a lady like you? You deserve a prince or a lord!"

"Stuff and nonsense!" laughed the princess. "To me you are both lord and prince!" The sound of her laughter was so full of joy, the fiddlers at once caught the key and broke into music as gay as a wedding.

Indeed that very night the time of their wedding was set!

Soon guests came from east, west, north, and from south. They made merry for eight days and nights. Castle and valley rang with their songs!

After that I cannot tell what happened for I stayed with them no longer.

The Christmas Bear

ONG ago in Norway up in Finnmark there lived a man whose name was Lars. His father's name had been Lars so the man in Finnmark was called Lars Larsson, or Son of Lars.

Lars had been out hunting and had trapped a large white polar bear and to her he gave the name of Freya.

About this time the king of Denmark sent out heralds to announce, "The man who brings His Majesty a tame white polar bear for Christmas can ask for anything and the king will grant the wish!"

This was music in the ears of Lars. He put a chain and a collar round Freya's neck and off they started for Denmark.

No one would take a live bear on cart or carriage, so the two had to go on foot. This made their travels long and hard, for snow lay deep and ice was thick on the roads.

As they journeyed south, the man and the bear had lost track of time, yet they sensed Christmas was drawing near for a gentle peace hung in the air and days were short as the sun waned.

About this time they reached the Dovre Mountains, which as everyone knows were once the home of trolls of every sort and size. The trolls used to hide in the

dark mountain caves and would come out only at night and then prowl abroad to frighten folk with their fiendish pranks.

When Lars and Freya came trudging through the mountain passes of Dovre, they were cold and hungry and longed for fire and food and shelter. As they passed between high cliffs they saw below, at the edge of the valley, a woodsman's cottage of brown logs. Blue smoke rose from the chimney.

"That looks like the home of honest folk," remarked Lars to the bear. "There we'll ask for food and shelter."

"I like my ice cave better. But you're master," grumbled the bear.

When they knocked at the door, a man with sad, blue eyes opened to them.

"We're on the way to the king of Denmark," began Lars. "He wants a live white bear for Christmas."

"You're rather late for that," growled the woodsman,

26

whose name was Halvor. "It's Christmas Eve tomorrow."

"Can we find food and shelter here?" went on Lars.

"We can't find it ourselves," mumbled the man half to himself.

"But at least you have the shelter of a home," said Lars, puzzled.

"This home tomorrow will be the home of trolls!" explained Halvor sadly. "Every Christmas Eve they come rolling down from the mountains and take possession of our cottage. Here they spend their feast days, taking from us the true Christmas spirit. Yet there is nothing we can do against them for they are far too strong." The man's eyes looked dark and troubled as he spoke.

To cheer him, Lars replied, "There is an old saying that when a stranger enters a house at Yuletide, he brings in good luck with him. There's no harm in letting me try!"

"No one can keep the trolls away," went on Halvor grimly. "But come in for a while and warm yourselves."

Lars and the white bear stepped into the house and soon were sitting snug and warm by the fire.

"Tell us about the trolls," said Lars as he looked round the cottage with its bright hand-woven hangings and bedcovers and its painted furniture and its old shiny bowls and plates.

"Each Christmas Eve from the mountain cave a pack of trolls troop down the slopes to find a place where they can hold their feast. No matter what we do the year round, on holy days the trolls return bringing wrack

27

and ruin with them and taking over our home! If you can free us from this evil, you can have whatever you desire in our house."

So it was agreed: the woodsman's family should quit the house on the morning of Christmas Eve, and then Lars and the white bear should move in.

The holy day passed under a soft silent snowfall. The mountains were white, the fields seemed blue with deep purple shadows from pine and spruce.

Stars seemed to twinkle and dance on the distant ice of the lake. All was peaceful and quiet over the valley and mountain slope. Not a troll was seen or heard.

In the woodsman's house was talk and firelight and warmth. Outdoors a sharp wind cried like a creature lost. The pines and the spruce moaned in the stillness.

"This is a strange kind of Christmas Eve! We should be dancing round the tree, and bringing in the yule log, and drinking the good mead, and eating the Christmas pig. Instead we're waiting for trolls in a strange house far from home and in a strange valley," said Lars to Freya.

"It's all because we went off to see the king of Denmark," grumbled the bear, and soon she was asleep with her nose in the ashes of the fireplace.

Lars went to one of the wall bunks and pulled aside the hand-woven curtain and climbed into bed, and pulled a reindeer fur over him for warmth. Soon he was fast asleep in the dark, still house.

There was no knowing what time Lars awakened, but suddenly he sat up in bed for he had heard a yelping and

a shouting and a crying as if a pack of wild animals were tumbling down the mountain slope.

Lars peered out from the tiny window next to his bunk, and saw against the moonlit snow, a great knot of black figures rushing toward the little hut.

Then Lars knew it was time to leap out of bed.

"Wake up, Freya, here come the trolls!" he cried.

The bear did not waken but slept on with her nose near the warm ashes, as if nothing at all was wrong with her world.

The yelling and yelping came close, ever closer. Lars could not keep himself from trembling.

"Wake up, Freya!" he repeated. "The trolls are here!" Lars shook the great white shoulder of the bear. She opened her eyes and gazed at him.

"Why fear trolls?" said she. "Don't you know a polar bear has the strength of twelve and the wit of one?" Freya stood up and stretched herself. She seemed to fill the whole room with her gleaming whiteness.

"No matter how strong or clever you are," Lars went on, "trolls are trolls! They are more and less than human for they have the strength of evil!"

Freya merely grunted and lay down again. This time she placed her huge form under the long table that stood in the shadows at the far end of the cottage.

Down the snowy slope the uproar grew louder and wilder. Soon the trolls were banging at the door. Lars leaped back into bed and drew the curtain to hide himself. Now the troll pack tore open the cottage and flooded in upon a torrent of darkness.

The trolls were a pack of wild creatures, half man and half beast. Some were as big as giants, others small as dogs. Some were humpbacked; some knock-kneed. There were noses as long as spades; and noses as round as hams. All had evil small eyes, hard and burning as live coals.

The oldest troll shouted, "Witch, bring in the feast!"

An eld-old witch with the face of tree bark rushed through the door followed by others of her kind. Presently they came back with sacks laden with troll food: dragons' tears mixed with seaweed, wolf hearts stewed in berries red as blood, and much more, far too horrible to relate.

In one corner of the hut, an old wizard wearing elk horns on his head began to beat upon a troll drum marked with magic signs.

When the witches had set the feast upon the long board, the troll pack gathered round, rubbing their paws, smacking their jaws, and patting their huge potbellies.

Now the troll pack set itself down to gorge, and then began a blood-curdling rending and tearing and gulping of food and drink.

Now the drum was beating louder and louder, and the trolls began to sing, but their singing seemed the screaming of eagles and the baying of wolves.

Lars trembled where he lay.

The troll feast went on and on. To Lars behind the curtain, the feast seemed to last a year and a day.

Suddenly one young troll picked up a bone and waving it in the air, cried out, "Where's the house pet

to gnaw this bone?" With that he ducked his head under the table and came up squealing with delight. He had caught sight of Freya lying under the board.

"Look at my big white cat!" the troll youngster shrieked. "It's the biggest in the whole world. Can I take it home to the caves?"

With that he tickled Freya's nose with the bone. The great bear shook herself. She began to growl.

With one movement of her immense body, Freya got to her feet. The table under which she had slept was lifted and knocked over with one swoop. The bear, white as a pillar of snow, stood erect on her hind legs and looked about with calm eyes. The house was hushed and not a creature moved. The trolls gaped in stony amazement at this towering beast.

Then Freya began to roar. Her voice was the sound of northern waters lashing against cliffs of ice. It echoed beyond the house roof as if there were no end to her thunder.

Now the bear stretched out her heavy white arms as if to crush the trolls to death in her embrace.

At once the evil creatures vanished into the night as if blown out by a northern gale. Over the snowy fields they rushed, and vanished into their mountain caves.

"So?" asked Freya, as she lay down again to warm her nose in the ashes. "What did I tell you?"

Lars said nothing but crept out from his wall bunk and began to put the house in order.

"Didn't I tell you it was good luck to take in a

stranger on Christmas Eve?" asked Lars when the woodsman's family returned next day to find peace and quiet once again master of the house.

"Now, Lars, since you've freed our home from evil spirits, stay to celebrate with us!"

So Lars stayed. And not long after, he wooed and wed the pretty daughter of the woodsman.

As for Freya, she went back to Finnmark. If you ever voyage far up into the North Sea, you may find some of her children's children riding upon the ice floes.

As for the king of Denmark, he never got a white polar bear for Christmas. But the Danes are a cheerful folk and no doubt their king received something else he liked just as well. Kings have a way of doing that.

Why the Bear's Tail Is So Short

N the forest one day Sir Michael, the fox, was slinking along with a large fish in his teeth. Bruin, the bear, met him and asked, "Where have you been today, Sir Fox?"

"Fishing," answered Sir Michael, dropping the fish but keeping one paw on it for he trusted no one, not even the stupid lumbering bear.

"Is fish good to eat like honey?" asked Mr. Bruin, sniffing the fish.

"Sweeter, and not full of bees," was the reply.

"If I want to go fishing what do I do?" bumbled the bear.

"Go to the lake, cut a hole in the ice, and drop your tail down into the water. Then wait!" grinned the fox.

"What for?" asked the big brown bear in his big bumbling way.

"Fish!" smirked the fox, and took to his heels with his dinner once more tight in his teeth.

Now in those days all bears had long tails which they waved after them like a bush.

So Bruin, the bear, waving his tail hopefully, lumbered through the tall pine trees down to an inland lake that was frozen tight. With much hard work and trouble, he cut a hole in the ice, sat down, and dropped his long tail through the hole into the cold water below.

Soon fish began to nibble on him.

"Each bite on *me* means more bites on *you* when I take you all home for supper!" burbled the bear.

The small fish did not answer.

A larger fish bit on the bear's tail.

"Are you herring or eel?" asked the bear.

The larger fish did not answer.

Suddenly came a long, strong pull.

"What are *you?*" roared the bear with tears in his eyes.

The largest fish did not answer.

"Are you dolphin or whale?"

Neither dolphin nor whale answered.

The bear was cold. The bear was sleepy. He slept. He forgot the fox, and the fish, and even his tail in the ice.

Suddenly the scream of a sea gull woke him. "Go home! Go home, while there's time!"

Bruin woke up with a start and tried to jump to his feet, but alas and alack he was frozen tight fast.

No matter, he thought, when I get loose I'll have enough fish to give me dinners for a month of Sundays!

With a great tug he pulled himself loose and turned to look round.

What did he find?

No fish and no tail, for the fish had bitten off his long bushy tail and had swum away with it into the deep waters.

And that is why, down to this very day, bears of every size and color and in every land have but a very small stub for a tail.

There ends my tale because the bear had so little.

The Pig That Went to Court

ONCE upon a time there lived a pig who was so tired of his board and bed that he sat in his pen and cried.

His three friends, the horse, the cow, and the cat gazed at him and asked him what his trouble was.

"All day long, all year long, I get nothing to eat but slops and scraps. By day I sit in the dust as you see; at night I sleep in wet mud. What kind of life is this for a pig?"

"Why not go out into the world and try your luck like anyone else?" neighed the horse.

"Luck may be bad or luck may be good," lowed the cow and gazed at the pig with her large wet eyes. "But still you can always try."

"Surely, it can't be any worse than it is," mewed the cat and washed her paws one after the other.

"Go up to the courthouse that stands on the hill," the three advised, "and ask the judge for a judgment to change your board and bed."

So little Mr. Pig dried his tears, polished the mud from his back, curled his tail, and set off for the courthouse.

"What have you to complain about?" asked the judge of the court. The judge was a large black raven with spectacles on his beak and a gray cape over his shoulders.

"Sir," replied the pig, "I'm so tired of my board and my bed that I want to change them both."

"Be satisfied with what you have," croaked the raven in a rusty voice.

"My friend, the horse, gets oats for his food," went on the pig. "My friend, the cow, eats grass; and the cat has her dish of milk. But for me, it's always the same: scraps and slops. As for a bed, always and ever, a bed of mud!"

The raven looked down his sharp beak and croaked, "Change is not good for man nor pig. But try a new life if you must. However, don't run back here if you don't like it."

"Oh, but I will like it," squealed the pig, turning red all over.

"From now on then," cawed the raven in his deepest voice, "for your board and bed you shall receive nothing but corn and peas, and you are condemned forever to sleep on a silken bed!"

When he heard this judgment, the pig was so happy he danced out of the courthouse, tripping over his own feet as he went.

He danced out of the town, away from the busy streets, and out into the country where he set off down the road which led to his home.

When he thought no one could hear him, he began to chant in small happy grunts, "Corn and peas, and a bed of silk!"

Little Mr. Pig, certain he was alone, was not aware that behind a clump of great rocks, Sir Michael, the fox, was sitting and grinning to himself and waiting to see what evil tricks he could play. When he caught sight of the pink piglet trotting happily along the road, he rubbed his paws together, and frisked his tail, and

laughed so large a laugh that he rolled over three times without stopping.

Slyly he began to listen to what Mr. Pig was grunting. "Corn and peas and a bed of silk! Corn and peas and a bed of silk!"

"I'll make you sing another song and that before long," jeered Sir Michael. So in a voice like an echo, the fox began to call, "Scraps and slops and a bed of mud! Scraps and slops and a bed of mud! Scraps and slops and a bed of mud!"

When he heard that sound, little Mr. Pig stopped short in his tracks and listened. His squint eyes looked around, and his tail uncurled, and his legs stuck fast in the dust. "That's funny!" he grunted. "Echo says 'scraps and slops and a bed of mud,' but the judge told me peas and corn and a bed of silk!" With a tangled look in his small eyes, he started trotting again and soon he had forgotten the echo and was grunting the happy song the raven had given him at the courthouse.

Carried on the wind again came that evil chant of the fox, "Scraps and slops and a bed of mud! Scraps and slops and a bed of mud!"

This time Mr. Pig stopped longer than before, and he listened with his small pointed ears twitching back and forth. "Why doesn't echo say what I say? What I say is: corn and peas and a bed of silk! Peas and silk and a bed of corn! Mud and corn and a bed of peas! No that's not right! But what was it? Scraps and peas and a muddy bed! No, that's not it either. Yes, I must begin all over again. Slops and peas and a bed of corn!"

Now the little pig sat down on his tail and started to cry because he couldn't remember what the raven had told him back in the courthouse.

All the while from behind the rocks came that wicked voice, "Scraps and slops and a bed of mud! Scraps and slops and a bed of mud!"

The little pig looked round at the dark trees. They were suddenly very dark. He gazed at the sky which had grown gray. He glanced at the rocks which looked sharper than ever he had known them. And he darted his eyes up and down the long way home that was so much longer than ever he had seen it before. He was afraid of everything. Afraid even of his own voice, so when he began to cry, "Peas and corn—" he broke off suddenly and said nothing more.

Instead he started to run, to run just as fast as his four short legs could carry him. All the while Sir Fox was bounding along from rock to rock and always out of sight. He was calling over and over again, "Slops and scraps and a bed of mud!"

Sir Fox was laughing to himself as the little pig kept on running and galloping along the road that grew darker and darker at every step.

After a long time, the piglet reached his home and trotted sadly into the barnyard where the horse and the cow and the cat were waiting for him.

"Well, what was the judgment?" they asked with one voice.

The pig sat down on his tail and said nothing. He was out of breath and out of joy too.

"Well?" they asked again.

Piglet looked at the ground. In a tired little grunt he

answered, "The judgment is: scraps and slops and a bed of mud!"

The three looked at their small friend in sorrow, but the little pig had forgotten them entirely, for he was rooting round in the dust as he had done so many times before, and as his father and his father's father had done before him, time without end.

The Rooster That Fell in the Brew Vat

NCE upon a time there lived a cock and a hen who went out into the grain field to pick up whatever they could find after the harvest, to kick up the dust, and to knock about.

All of a sudden, the hen lit upon a barleycorn and the cock turned up a hop cone. Then and there they decided to make some malt and to brew their Christmas ale.

"I pick up barley and I make malt and I brew ale and ale is good!" cackled the hen.

"Is the malt mixture good and strong?" asked the cock as he flew up to the edge of the vat, for he wanted to taste the liquid. But when he was about to bend over to take a drop, he flapped his wings so many times he fell on his head into the brew vat and there he drowned.

When the hen saw what had happened to her husband, she lost her mind and flew straight to the chimney shelf, and cackled in one breath as if she never would stop, "Help! Help! Help! He's been hurt and he's dead! Help! Help! Help! He's dead and been hurt!"

"What's biting you, hen? Why do you carry on so?" asked the little hand mill that was standing close by.

"Didn't you see my old man fall in the brew vat and

drown? He lies dead and that's why I grieve and groan!" cackled the hen on and on.

"I'm sorry to hear that, so I'd better start grinding and cutting at once!" murmured the mill. And this he did.

When the chair saw and heard this, he asked, "What's eating you, mill? Why do you grind and cut up like mad?"

"Didn't you see old man rooster fall in the brew vat and drown? Don't you know his wife sits on the shelf and grieves? So I have to grind and cut up like mad!" With this the mill went on turning faster than before.

"If that's how you take it, I'd better start creaking and cracking at once," squeaked the chair. And this he did.

When the door saw what took place, he asked, "What's bothering you, chair? Why do you crack and creak like that?"

The chair replied, "Didn't you see old man rooster fall in the brew vat and drown? Don't you know his hen perches on the wall shelf and grieves? Can't you hear the mill grinding like mad? For these sad reasons I have to creak and to crack the life out of me!" And this he did.

Then the door flew open and slammed itself shut, and cried, "If everything and everyone grieves and groans, what can I do but rattle and bang?"

And this he did, making such a noise everyone in the house felt it both in marrow and bone.

When the kindling bin full of chips and sawdust heard what went on, he asked of the door, "Why do you rattle and bang so? You'll knock your hinges out if you keep on like this!"

The door only slammed again and answered, "You ought to know the rooster fell in the brew vat and drowned. See his wife grieve on the shelf! Listen to the hand mill turning like mad! Hear the chair creaking and cracking! As for me, I'm so sad I must rattle and bang till the whole house shakes!"

The bin thought for a moment, then replied, "Well if that's the state we're in, I'll scatter my chips and saw-dust as fast as I can!" And this he did until the whole room seemed lost in a fog.

Suddenly the rake that leaned against the window on

the outside of the farmhouse asked the bin, "What's all this silly scattering and blowing round about?"

To which the bin answered, "Mercy on us! Haven't you seen the cock fall in the vat and drown? Heard the hen grieve on the shelf? Watched the mill grind everything into small bits and pieces? Noticed the chair creak and crack, and the door rattle and bang? What can I do but scatter sawdust and chips?"

To which the rake muttered, half to itself, "What a scoundrel I'd be if I didn't grieve too! I know what I'll do! I'll rake and I'll rend everything in sight!" And this he did, so the farmyard seemed a cloud of flying grass and leaves.

These curious happenings were noticed by the aspen tree in the garden.

"Tell me, what is this foolish raking and rending?" asked the tree calmly.

The rake stopped for a moment to answer. "The rooster drowned in the vat. The hen perches high on the shelf. The mill grinds and cuts. The chair creaks and cracks. The door slams and bangs. The kindling bin scatters. Don't I have to show my grief somehow? What else can I do but rake and rend everything in sight?"

"If you must, you must," sighed the tree gently and then began to ponder and brood what it could do to show its sympathy for the poor foolish rooster that had fallen into the brew vat and drowned.

Soon the tree spoke again. "I can do nothing better than to sorrow with all my lovely leaves." And this she did until the fields and meadows heard a soft music of

sorrow from the aspen tree and knew it was not caused by the wind for the air was calm and still.

The birds of the wood and field heard this whispering and murmuring, and soon they came flocking and asked, "Aspen, why do you make such sweet sad music with your lovely leaves?"

To which the tree replied, "Alas, our poor friend, the rooster, was too greedy for ale and thus he fell in the vat and drowned. Alas, for his wife who lost her mind and flew to the shelf to grieve forever. Alas, for the mill grinding for grief, and the chair creaking his loss. The door bangs for sorrow, and the bin scatters because of misery. The rake cannot stand still for heartbreak. I, too, must show sorrow, and thus it is my leaves mourn and whisper in the wind!"

Hearing all this, the birds began to twitter and chirp, "Then we must be sad too! But what shall we do? Ah yes, we can pull the feathers from our breasts and toss them to the four winds so the whole world will learn of the fate of our poor friend, the rooster!"

Soon the garden was full of flying feathers, for the four winds loved to toss and to lift them in the summer air.

These strange happenings were seen by the farmer as he was standing on the threshold of his cottage. When he saw the feathers whirling about the farmyard and heard the mad twittering of the birds, he cried, "You foolish little birds! Why do you pick and pluck your feathers out of your breasts and toss them to the four winds?"

To which the birds replied, "Rooster drowned. Hen grieves. Mill grinds. Chair creaks. Door bangs. Bin scatters. Rake rends. Aspen shivers. Being many, we sorrow more than others. We tear our feathers from our breasts. We toss them to the four winds!"

The farmer thought for a moment while his glance rested on the old broom that stood near the door. Loudly he shouted, "You have all done your grieving in your own way. What is now left for a man to do but to tear this old broom to pieces and to scatter the twigs both east and west?"

This noise and nonsense was seen and heard by the farm wife, busy cooking the evening porridge. When she saw her husband tear their one and only broom to pieces, she screamed, "Is that a way for a grown man to

act? How can I sweep the house tomorrow if you tear our last and only broom to pieces?"

But the farmer only tore more twigs from the broom as he shouted back, "Woman, don't you listen to gossip? Our cock has just fallen into our Christmas ale and ruined it. Our hen broods on the shelf where she has no business to be. Our mill that won't grind for me now grinds for a rooster. Our chair creaks its nails out! Our door bangs its hinges loose! Our kindling bin darkens our house! Our rake tears up grass and bush. Our tree won't keep quiet for a minute! Our birds fill the air with feathers. Since all these terrible things happen to us, what else can I do but tear up the last broom, for surely the end of the world is come!"

The old woman stood stock still for some time. Then tears filled her eyes and she cried, "If my cock drowned and my hen grieves and my mill grinds and my chair creaks and my door bangs and my bin scatters and my tree shivers and my birds pull feathers and *you* tear our last and only broom to pieces, what is left for an old woman to do that no one else has thought of doing?"

"Well, what?" shouted the farmer hoarsely.

"Why, smear house and roof with porridge!" was her reply. And at once she began to carry out her plan so in no time at all, kitchen and house walls and even the roof were smeared so thick with porridge no one could see how the house was made.

As far as I know, she may be smearing it still. I have not been there to look.

The Hen That Saved the World

NCE upon a time there was a hen named Mistress Penny. She lived in a deep mountain valley in Norway, and at the far end of that valley was a high mountain called Dovre.

One night, Penny flew up into an oak tree to roost. There she sat all night, and there she dreamed a dream.

And the dream was this: if she did not get up to Dovre Mountain at once then the whole wide world would surely come to an end!

Though the sun was not yet up, Penny flew from the tree and set off at once down the road that led to the mountain called Dovre.

When she had gone a little way she met the rooster known as Booster.

"Good day, Mr. Booster," said the hen.

"Good day, Mistress Penny," replied the rooster. "Where are you going so early in the day?"

"I'm going to Dovre Mountain so the whole wide world won't come to an end," answered the hen.

"But who told you the world would come to an end?"

"Last night I sat in an oak tree and dreamed it," explained Penny.

"If that's so," crowed the rooster, "I'll save the world too!" So he started off after the hen.

Hopping and running and running and hopping, they set off down the road. After some time, they met a duck whose nickname was Lucky.

"Good day, Sir Lucky!" began the rooster.

"Good day to you! But where are you going so early in the morning?" asked the duck.

"I was going to Dovre Mountain so the world won't come to an end," replied the rooster.

"But who told you the whole world would come to an end?"

"Mistress Penny told me so," explained the rooster.

"And who told you that?" asked the duck.

"I sat in an oak tree and dreamed it," answered Penny and shook her feathers.

"I'll join you then," quacked the duck and dropped into line. And so Penny the hen, Booster the rooster, and Lucky the duck all set off for the mountain called Dovre so that the whole wide world would not come to an end!

After these three had run, hopped, and waddled on for a stretch of road, they met a goose whose nickname was Woosie.

"Good day to you, Woosie," said the duck who was the last of all and so had more time to stop and talk.

"Good day, Lucky," said the goose, "where are you all going so early in the morning?"

"Oh, we're all going to Dovre so the world won't come to an end!" quacked the duck.

"Who told you this news?" inquired the goose.

"Booster told me."

"Who told you, Booster?"

"Penny told me!"

"How do you know, Penny, that the world is coming to an end?" honked Woosie.

"Last night in an oak tree I sat and dreamed it," cackled the hen and shook her feathers.

"Well, I don't want our world to come to an end so I might as well go along too," honked the goose and stepped into line behind Lucky, who was waddling after Booster, who was hopping and running on the heels of Penny, who was tripping along as fast as she could so the whole wide world would not come to an end!

When this parade had gone a long way down the road, they met a fox, who saw through everything, even keyholes, so his name was Locksy.

"Good day, Locksy!" called the goose who was behind the others and so had more time to stop and chat.

"Good day to you, Woosie!" smiled the fox, "and where are you waddling so early in the morning?"

"Oh, haven't you heard? We're all going to Dovre to keep the whole wide world from coming to an end!"

"Who told you that silly story?" smiled the fox.

"Lucky told me."

"Who told Lucky?"

"Why, Booster, of course!"

"Booster, where did you hear that foolish story?" The fox smiled more and more so that his sharp and cold teeth shone between his dark jaws.

"Why, haven't you heard?" cackled Penny. "Only last night I sat in an oak tree and dreamed that if I didn't go to Dovre Mountain at once, then the whole wide world would come to an end!"

As the hen finished this speech, she ruffled her feathers still more, and gazed at the fox gravely.

"Rubbish!" laughed the fox. "The world won't come to an end if you don't get to Dovre this morning or any morning. Come along to my house. There it's warm and snug, and you won't know if the world comes to an end or not."

Soon they all were following the fox home to his den. When they got there, the fox built up his fire so the place became as warm as an oven and nearly as snug.

Then the hen, the rooster, the duck, and the goose began to feel sleepy.

The duck and the goose perched in a corner; but the rooster and the hen flew up high and perched on a rafter.

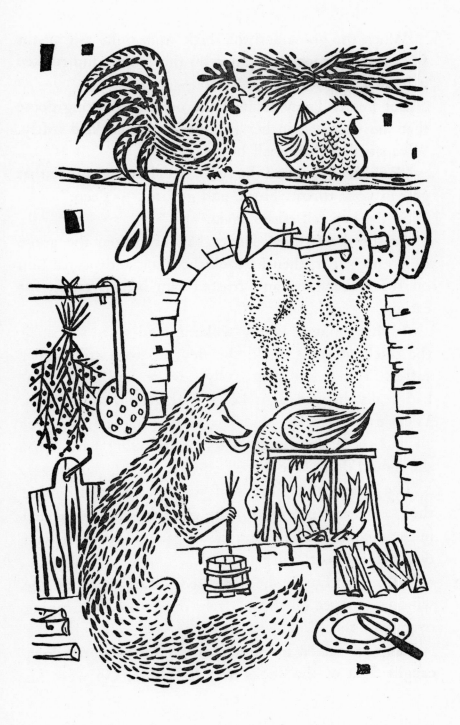

When the goose and the duck were quite asleep, the fox took the goose and put it on the embers and roasted it brown.

But Penny knew so well the odor of roasting goose that she wakened in her half-sleep, and cackled softly, "I've smelled that smell before . . ."

"Rubbish," laughed the fox. "It's chimney smoke that gets in your throat. Hush, and go back to sleep."

So the hen fell asleep again.

As for the fox, no sooner had he gotten the goose down his gullet, then he took the duck and placed him on the embers too and roasted him brown ready for eating.

At that moment Penny woke up and when she smelt the smell of roast duck, she flew up to a still higher rafter. When she was fully awake and saw what had really happened to her old traveling companions, Woosie and Lucky, she flew to the highest rafter of all and there she clung in terror, thinking hard what she should do to save herself and her friend, the rooster.

The sound of hundreds of wings was heard outside the house, and peering up the chimney, Penny beheld in the moonlight the gleam of wings and breasts of wild ducks flying past.

"Oh, Mr. Fox," she screamed. "Look out of the window and see all those lovely duck suppers escaping over your roof!"

The fox darted his beady eye out of the window, caught sight of the ducks over his house. Up went his

tail in glee, out he darted from his house to catch still
more supper.

"Wake up, Booster, and save your life! No time to
be lost! No time to be lost!" cackled Penny in a flutter
of feathers and fear.

Booster unloosed his head from under his wing,
looked sharply at Penny for waking him up so rudely.

"Mr. Fox has eaten our friends and if you don't
hurry he'll eat you too!"

"But where is he now?" sputtered the rooster, look-
ing down from his rafter into the room which glowed
with firelight and smelt strongly of roast goose and
duck.

"He's out catching more supper," snapped Penny
quickly. "Now I hear him . . . he's coming back!"

And to be sure he was. But a very sad fox was he

with nary a duck in his paw or maw and only an empty house to welcome him.

For Mistress Penny and Mr. Booster had flown up the chimney and far out over the valley.

And if they had not flown straight to the mountain called Dovre just as Penny had dreamed in the oak tree the night before, then as everybody knows, the world would surely have come to an end!